Max Stravinsky

Crêpes Suzette

Leon Kampinsky

Ferrrnando Extra Debonnaire

in

MAX IN HOLLYWOOD, BABY

A BELLA BROCCOLI/D.B. DARLING PRODUCTION

Based on an idea by Leon Kampinsky

From a concept by Marcel Proust

Maliciously stolen by Ivan Kazlinsky from Truman Capote

at a martini drenched lunch, Le Côte Basque, December 1952

WRITTEN AND DIRECTED BY MAIRA KALMAN

Production design	M&Co.
Special effects and stunt coordination	EMILY OBERMAN
Hair and makeup	MISS KEIRA ALEXANDRA OSIPOV
Merengue sequence choreographed by	KIRSTEN COYNE
Key Grip	DIDDO RAMM
Edited, edited and edited again by	NANCY PAULSEN
Role of Swifty Lazar played by	CHARLOTTE SHEEDY
Catering	SARA BERMAN
Best Boy	ALEXANDER T. KALMAN
Spiritual Advisor	LULU
Lawsuits pending	MAURICE CHAGALL v. LEON KAMPINSKY
	FEDERICO DE POTATOES v. FERRRNANDO EXTRA DEBONNAIRE
	BELLA BROCCOLI v. D.B. DARLING
	MAX STRAVINSKY v. MAIRA KALMAN
Silent partners and laundered money provided by	THE NEW YORK REVIEW CHILDREN'S COLLECTION

ISBN 978-1-68137-234-1; ebook ISBN 978-1-68137-235-8

Copyright © Maira Kalman, 1992
All rights reserved

Library of Congress Cataloging-in-Publication Data
Names: Kalman, Maira, author, illustrator.
Title: Max in Hollywood, baby / by Maira Kalman.
Description: New York : New York Review Books, [2018] | Series: New York
   Review children's collection | Summary: When Max the millionaire poet dog
   and his Parisian poodle bride Crêpes Suzette leave Paris for the lure of
   glittering Hollywood, can movie stardom be far behind?
Identifiers: LCCN 2017034894| ISBN 9781681372341 (hardback) | ISBN
   9781681372358 (epub)
Subjects: | CYAC: Motion pictures—Production and direction—Fiction. |
   Dogs—Fiction. | Hollywood (Los Angeles, Calif.)—Fiction. | Humorous
   stories. | BISAC: JUVENILE FICTION / Animals / Dogs. | JUVENILE FICTION /
   Humorous Stories. | JUVENILE FICTION / Imagination & Play.
Classification: LCC PZ7.K1256 May 2018 | DDC [E]—dc23
LC record available at https://lccn.loc.gov/2017034894

Printed in U.S.A.   10 9 8 7 6 5 4 3 2 1

This is a New York Review Book
Published by The New York Review of Books
435 Hudson Street
New York, NY 10014

THE PRODUCERS GRATEFULLY ACKNOWLEDGE THE INVALUABLE ASSISTANCE OF THE FOLLOWING:
The Institute for Advanced Study, Princeton, New Jersey
The Izmir of Zim Zum
Bureau of Cosmetology, Forbidden City, Peking

Filmed on location

"the izmir of zimzum is dizzy for your fish izzy"

I used to
be just Max.
Poet. Plodder.
Pickleface.
Now I'm in Hollywood
directing a movie.
How did I get here?
On Leon Kampinsky's
beautiful **no**se.
But I might as well
begin at the beginning . . .

[FLASHBACK] to interior of lavish New York apartment. I had just returned from Paris with my bride Crêpes Suzette. The fish clock on the mantel had barely chimed midnight, when a persistent buzzzbuzzz of the buzzer heralded the arrival of a telegram.

ZIPO ⚡ GRAM

DEAR MAXIE AND CREPES STOP
WHERE ARE YOU STOP STOP
STOPPING UP THE WORKS STOP
START AT ONCE STOP STOP
SHILLYSHALLYING AROUND STOP
STOP WASTING TIME STOP START
PACKING STOP PULLING OUT ALL
THE STOPS STOP START
STOP START STOP START STOP
LOVE LEON

Were these the
ravings of a madman
or an agent?   **BOTH!**
It was the cigar chomping angel himself,
beckoning us to Hollywood where deals grow on vines.
I was to write and direct a movie. Crêpes was to compose the score.

[CUT] to nervous interlude.
Close-up on Max.
Could this dog handle it?
It's no picnic if you try
something and fail.
What if they make a
monkey out of me?
What if they smell a rat?

Wait.
I'm no chicken.
I can do this. I will do this.
California, here I come.

At the airport we were met by a snappy chappy:

"My name is
Ferrrnando
Extra Debonnaire.

"I have studied at the
Royal Academy of Driving Director
My face drives them wild,
my directing will drive them mad,
but in the meantime, I just drive.
Life is full of surpreezes, no?
Welcome to L.A. Hop in the stretch.
Are you wearing stretch pants?"

"Watch your step in this town.
There are some back-stabbing,
power-hungry, status-seeking
vegetarians here.
I know of what I speak.
But hey, let's d r i i i v e.
If someplace is close
that means you only drive for
twenty or thirty hours with
your eyes peeled for stars and with
your mouth glued to the phone
yackin and yammerin about
this deal or that script and
faster than you can say
'Marcello Mastroianni
likes to eat salami,'
you have arrived."

We arrived at our hotel. The Garden of Allah. We stood entranced in the midst of a flowering perfumed paradise. Jasmine, honeysuckle, climbing roses. Lemons as big as footballs. Bougainvillea arching up into the turquoise sky.

A fountain sprinkled, birds chirped, swans glided.

A bellhop showed us into the Hubba-Hubba Suite.
He flashed us a smile and started to sing:

"Anything you want sir, anything at all
Just press this golden button and give me a call.
You used to be a nobody, an isn't, a not
And now you are a big deal, a someone, a shot.
You used to be a nebbish, a noodle, a fool
And now you're Mr. Big Time with your own private pool.
No order too tall. No excess that can vex us.
We'll treat you like a king, as long as you're a winnah
But if your flick's a flop you'll be whistling for your dinnah."

And with that he tap-danced out of the room.

"Max,"
Crêpes smiled sultrily,
"you know
how to wheestle,
don't you?"

I went to find Leon at poolside. Easier said than do

Pages were pacing around paging people. "Pagin

Mr. Popofski." "PAGING MRS

TUTUTSKI." "Mr. Wiseguy, M

Wisenheimer loves the script." "MR. WISEAC

MR. WISECRACK THINKS THE SCRIPT SMELLS

LIKE A THREE DAY FISH." At long last I found Leon.

Leon, this life is so lush, so luscious, so luscious-wuscious."

Can the poetry," Leon interrupted. "Save it for the Big

Cheese. They are waiting for us at the studio. Let's go, Maxie."

Back in the car Ferrrnando was rehearsing his directing.
"Baby, could you put more pizzazz in that?" and

"Darling,   the camera is not liking you today."

"Yow," he shrieked,   "there goes Katharine Hepburn."

It was some trip. We made a right at the giant hat

. . . and a left at the humongous hot dog and there we were . . .

. . . at the gates of Megalomania Studios.
I stared, mesmerized.
Movies . . . A darkened theater.
A raspberry velvet seat. A bag of popcorn.
What more could you ask for?

I'm crazy for movies
I'm weak at the knees
English mysteries,
screwball comedies
Spaghetti westerns
three bowls please
It doesn't matter what, it doesn't matter who
If it's Fred Astaire and Ginger Rogers
It'll absolutely do I worship their allure
If I'm sick, don't find a cure
A Hitchcock scream, a Fellini dream
Film noir, Mel Blanc
And all that's in between
Flood my senses
Make me weep
Kiss the heroine
Kill the creep
The credits, the edits
Houdini! Whodunnits!
Musicals that dance
And dancicals that muse
I'm filled with hope watching Cinemascope
Cause I'm no dope
I love movies.

A booming voice slapped me back to earth:
"WHO WISHES TO PASS THESE PORTALS, SOME MERE MORTALS?
WHAT IS THE SECRET PASSWORD?" the voice demanded.
"Swordfish?" I ventured.
Faster than you could say "star-struck starlet with a seven year itch,"
the gates swung open, and I breezed in like King Vidor.

Feeling as chipper as a kipper I strolled into the white-white room where a secretary was answering ten phones a mile a minute.

"HELLO. No can do. three? HELLO. HELLO. That's a hot tip. Please send up a fluke. HELLO. He wants a cello. HELLO. Just sack that fellow. HELLO. He will. HELLO. He won't. HELLO. He's mad. HELLO. He's livid. HELLO. He says the sky's the limit. HELLO. HELLO. Where have you gone to? HELLO. HELLO. Just get it PRONTO. Hello. GOODBYE. And here's a clue. Don't call us, we'll call you."

HELLO. He won't see you. HELLO. Lunch at It's not up to me. HELLO. It's just gossip. HELLO. Dinner with the Duke. HELLO.

She gave me the fish eye.
"You're no Spencah Tracy," she drawled, "but Mr. Darling will see you now."

D.B. Darling

The biggest Darling of them all. Leon and I cringed into the room. But it wasn't a room. It was a **fish**. A roomy fish. A fishy room. A big fat blue fish, a carp to be exact. And like the innocent Pinocchio with his Jiminy Kampinsky, we walked into the mouth of this fish. But this fish was full of water and in the middle, drifting in a canoe, was D.B. and his crew.

Holy mogul!

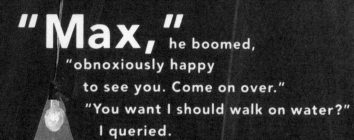

"Max," he boomed,
"obnoxiously happy
to see you. Come on over."
"You want I should walk on water?"
I queried.
"Ixnay on the isecrackway,"
Leon growled.
"Just smile and swim."
We swam over and soggily sat
in the canoe.
"Max, we want you to
write us a movie.
A sugar-smackin,
rootin-tootin, high-spy, sci-fi,
kissy-kissy,
melt-in-your-mouth,
madcap musical mystery.
A box-office banana—
I mean bonanza.

"Can you deliver?"
"Can a snake slither?"
snapped Leon. "Fabuloso. But
before you leave I want you to
meet your yes-man, Bernie Bennie
and your yes-man's yes-man, Diddo."
"A yes-man?" I smirked in disbelief. "A
yes-man's yes-man?" "Max," D.B. inter-
jected while uncorking a bottle of Chateau-
Neuf de Pup, "a yes-man is indispensable
in this town and, as everyone knows, two
yesses are better than one. Let's toast to that.

EGOS UP."

Outside in the blinding light I felt dizzy. What was that lunatic talking about? "Ferrrnando, do you know any good hideaways? I'm totally confused." "There's Cafe Kafka, Mecca for the Miserable. But you know what Shakespeare said, 'Don't kvetch in the stretch.' Look, you're no Einstein (or Eisenstein, for that matter), but ya havetahavehope."

PSST, HEY BUB, YA WANNA BUY A SCRIPT, CHEAP?

Ferrrnando was right.
I needed a heavenly slice of hope.
I needed CHEESECAKE.
We zoomed to Cheesecake of the Stars where the hoi polloi hobnob with hopefuls and muckety mucks seduce swanky stars.

I wolfed down the Carole Lombard raspberry cheesecake. I polished off a slice of Gary Cooper. My stomach was full, but my head was empty.

Back in the car driving around I saw a billboard:

HOW   SHOULD

A PLOT TO MAKE THEM PLOTZ YOU DON'T GOTZ?
CALL MADAME GIZELKA
★ Psychic to the Stars ★

I   KNOW

"Ferrrnando," I yelped, "Madame Gizelka's and step on it."
"Faster than you can say 'Fasten your seatbelt, it's going to be a bumpy night,' I will get you there."

I entered Gizelka's gossamer chamber.

"Hello," I meekly squeaked, "I am. . ."

"No need for introductions, droopy face. I am a psychic. And **you** are a dog in hot water. Listen, tootsie, you're no Orson Welles, but I can help you.

"You're looking for an idea, but are you barking up the wrong tree! In this town all you need are big feet and a hot head...I mean hot feet and a big head...I mean flat feet and a hole in your head...I mean ...oh never mind." She took a pair of yellow gloves and a giant headdress out of a blue box. "Wear these and your power will knock the toupees right off their heads." The next thing I know she vanishes in a puff of smoke, chanting, "Lassie, Asta, Sparky, this pooch is feeling yucky, I've worked my magic malarkey and now he will be lucky."

Back at the hotel, reactions were mixed.

"Good grief," said Leon. "Why are you wearing a popcorn bucket on your head?" "Dashing wardrobe, darling," smiled Crêpes. "I love it madly," gushed Bernie. "Ditto," gushed Diddo. "This," I explained mystically, "is my magic out-fit. Call me Mr. Lucky." "I call you Mr. Idiot," Leon retorted. "Leon, any-one can be normal. But to be an idiot. Now, that's something."

LESS IS MORE. BABY

"Max," Crêpes looked at me pointedly. "be carefool." "Of what?" I asked, admiring myself in the mirror. "Of ze big banana peel, of ze cream pie in your face. Beware."

K

ME

And so I was ready to write. But there were so many distractions. Massages. Manicures.

omatherapy. Acupuncture. Personal trainers. Power lunches. Waterfalls of mineral water.

I met my producer **Bella Broccoli**
who insisted we drink a
brussels sprouts and sauerkraut shake
("the secret of youth, darling")
before each meeting.
We were feted at hotsy-totsy parties
where the swimming pools were
filled with ice cream and
the trees were made out of chocolate.
I was interviewed by
the gossip columnist Billy Sandwich
who linked me romantically
(and ridiculously, I might add)

with Monica Zitti, the tantalizing starlet, who was breathlessly
quoted as saying, "I admire his boots—I mean his books."
I bought art. I played tennis and polo and
rode Arabian horses on the beach and
after all this terribly hard work,
I produced a script.

Bernie read it and wept with admiration.
 Ditto Diddo.
 I showed it to Crêpes,
who was furiously practicing the Bach Carpaccios.
"Max, eet ees flimsy, and superficial.
 Zee women are cardboard, zee men are morons.
 Zer eez not a soupçon of wit,
  no humor, no soul, no intelligence."
   "But Crêpes, do you like it?" I asked hopefully.
    "Max, eet will lay ze big oeuf."
     "You are wrong," I growled. "This script is **perfect**."

> **"Perfect,"** sighed Bernie.
> **"Ditto,"** dithered Diddo.

VELMA

VIV

So I started to make my movie. When the script is written, you search the globe for the star. That is called casting. When you have found the absolutely perfect person in every way, you have to change them over *completely*. That is called the makeover. You take a Velma Levine and transform her into *Vivi Divine*. Then the costumes need to be designed. Gowns made from silk illusion. Organza. Plumes. Strapless wonders. Flaring skirts. Tempers flaring. Fittings. Sittings.

Endless, endless, endless meetings.

We're over budget, we're under stress
And all the time they ask of you,
"Mr. Stravinsky, what should we do?
Do you want this, do you want that?
How should we do it? What should we get?"
And all I can think is:

I want more, more, more!

I want pink walls of quilted satin.

I want fresh bagels from Manhattan.

I want more pom-poms on that hat.

I want six legs on that cat.

I want a monogrammed cravat

That says Stravinsky Thought of That.

I want to pout and rant and rave

and get everything I crave

I want to be a celebrity

Have my pawprints in cement for posterity

And just when it seems I have all that I adore

I will graciously implore: I want more I want more I want more.

I won't have conversations, I'll just have monologues.

I won't be simply human. I'll be a demigod.

I will be so eccentric, and they'll still be sycophantic

I will give my opinions to all my harrassed minions

Like King Tut with all his plunder,

just like him, how I will thunder

give me more give me more give me more.

I want the whole world to love me

Is that asking very much?

Like the lion in the jungle who devours all his prey

I will tear limb from limb all those who won't obey

and from my gilded throne (which I simply call "just home")

I will regally intone

I want more I want more I want more!

I was broken from my
reverie by a phone call.
Crêpes was waiting for me
at the Waco Taco.

I was ravenous!
"Let me have

two taco tamales

tamales tacquitos

tacquitos burritos

burritos peppito

and make it **speedito**."

Crêpes was looking at me funny.
"What's wrong, Crêpes?"
"Max, eezer your hat eez shrinking or
your head eez getting bigger."
"That's ridiculous, Crêpes.
It couldn't be. Could it?"

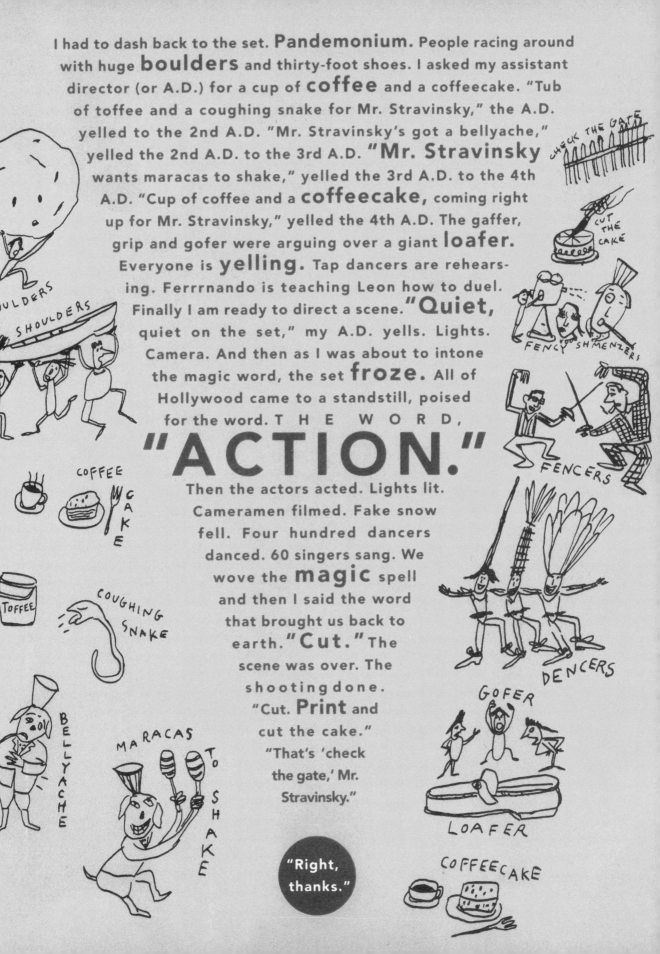

I had to dash back to the set. **Pandemonium.** People racing around with huge **boulders** and thirty-foot shoes. I asked my assistant director (or A.D.) for a cup of **coffee** and a coffeecake. "Tub of toffee and a coughing snake for Mr. Stravinsky," the A.D. yelled to the 2nd A.D. "Mr. Stravinsky's got a bellyache," yelled the 2nd A.D. to the 3rd A.D. "**Mr. Stravinsky** wants maracas to shake," yelled the 3rd A.D. to the 4th A.D. "Cup of coffee and a **coffeecake,** coming right up for Mr. Stravinsky," yelled the 4th A.D. The gaffer, grip and gofer were arguing over a giant **loafer.** Everyone is **yelling.** Tap dancers are rehearsing. Ferrrnando is teaching Leon how to duel. Finally I am ready to direct a scene. "**Quiet,** quiet on the set," my A.D. yells. Lights. Camera. And then as I was about to intone the magic word, the set **froze.** All of Hollywood came to a standstill, poised for the word. T H E W O R D,

"ACTION."

Then the actors acted. Lights lit. Cameramen filmed. Fake snow fell. Four hundred dancers danced. 60 singers sang. We wove the **magic** spell and then I said the word that brought us back to earth. "**Cut.**" The scene was over. The shooting done. "Cut. **Print** and cut the cake." "That's 'check the gate,' Mr. Stravinsky."

"Right, thanks."

BOULDERS

SHOULDERS

COFFEE CAKE

TOFFEE

COUGHING SNAKE

BELLYACHE

MARACAS TO SHAKE

CHECK THE GATE

CUT THE CAKE

FENCY SHMENZERS

FENCERS

DENCERS

GOFER

LOAFER

COFFEECAKE

The next day nobody could do anything right.

Someone told the dancers to **break a leg** and they all broke their legs.

Vivi had **laryngitis** from screaming at her manager; the stunt monkey was threatening to quit unless he got a bigger trailer.

Vino Valentino the heartthrob **fell off** the balcony and started speaking in Chinese.

Ferrrnando was teaching Leon the merengue (which was driving me **insane-gue)** and to top it off, Crêpes was glowering because I said her music was not so hot.

I lay down on my cot. The string quartet I had hired to soothe me played. I dozed off. But the dream was really terrifying. I dreamed that I was in the middle of a vast hall and that everything was falling down around me and I was on a wild horse and that these grotesque gremlins were stomping toward me chanting . . .

"Your head is getting fatter
your ego's on a ladder

going up up up

you great conceited pup
you have nerves of steel
and an iron will
who do you think you are,
Cecil B. de Mille?
Your movie's a disaster
and it's all because of you
The papers will review it
and yell,
'POOCH'S PIC P.U.'"

Text inside the donut illustration:

I jumped up with a yelp. Crêpes was right. My head was the size of a watermelon. The movie was a disaster. What kind of jerk had I become? "A schlemiel," Crêpes (who had obviously been talking to Leon) supplied when she came in. "You have become ze insufferable show-business schmendrick. And you know what? I think we should end zis book right here. Ferrrnando can fix zis fiasco. We must get away from ze madness. And Max, I have something to tell you. . ."

EINSTEIN'S DONUTS

Try our box of BLACK HOLES

I was me again.
I looked at Crêpes, cross-eyed with love.
The sky was vast. The night was clear.
I felt on the brink of a grand adventure.
What could it be?

"Yes, yes and yes,"
yessed Bernie. "I don't
agree," said Diddo. "What do you
mean, you don't agree?" "What do
you mean, what do I mean? I'm not sure
that in the big picture that life is full of
surprises. Perhaps everything is foretold."
"Are you saying that fate or some omniscient
being controls our lives? That's ridiculous."
"No, it's not. I would refer you to Schopenhauer and
his treatise *The World as Will and Representation*, in
which he clearly—" "Not the Schopenhauer again, you're
giving me a headache. If I'm wrong, then you have to be
wrong. Wrong, wrong and forever wrong." "You are wrong
infinity." "You are wrong to the utmost extension of pi."
ou are wronger than the outfit my Aunt Edith
re to Hilda's engagement party." "I can't top that."

Life is full of surpreezes, no?